# Curious George®
## Plants a Seed

# Jorge el curioso
# siembra una semilla

Adaptación de Erica Zappy
Traducido por Yanitzia Canetti
Basado en un guión para una serie de televisión
escrito por Sandra Willard

Houghton Mifflin Company
Boston 2007

Adaptation by Erica Zappy
Translated by Yanitzia Canetti
Based on the TV series teleplay written by Sandra Willard

For information about permission to reproduce selections from this book, write to Permissions, Houghton Mifflin Company, 215 Park Avenue South, New York, New York 10003.

Library of Congress Cataloging-in-Publication data is on file.

Design by Joyce White

www.houghtonmifflinbooks.com

Manufactured in China
WKT 10 9 8 7 6 5 4 3 2 1

Jumpy Squirrel was very busy.
George was curious.
What was Jumpy doing?

La ardilla Saltarina estaba muy ocupada.
Jorge sintió curiosidad.
¿Qué estaba haciendo Saltarina?

Bill, the boy next door, told George,
"Jumpy buries acorns and nuts.
He stores them in the ground.

Beto, el vecino de Jorge, le dijo:
—Saltarina entierra bellotas y nueces.
Ella las almacena bajo tierra.

He can dig them
up later, when he is
hungry."

**Y puede sacarlas después,
cuando tenga hambre.**

That gave George
a great idea!
George buried
the orange juice.

**Esto le dio a Jorge
¡una gran idea!
Enterró el jugo de naranja.**

He buried the butter.
He buried the bread.
He was glad to find a
good place to store food.

**Enterró la mantequilla.**
**Enterró el pan.**
**Y estaba feliz de haber hallado un**
**buen lugar para almacenar la comida.**

When the man with the yellow hat came home, the kitchen was empty!

Cuando el hombre del sombrero amarillo llegó a casa, ¡la cocina estaba vacía!

Where was all of their food?

¿Dónde estaba toda su comida?

George proudly showed his friend.

**Jorge señaló hacia afuera orgullosamente.**

"George, orange juice and bread are not
for burying," the man with the yellow hat said.
"They cannot be stored in the ground."

—¡Pero Jorge!, el jugo de naranja y el pan
no se entierran —dijo el hombre del sombrero amarillo—.
No se pueden almacenar bajo tierra.

His friend showed George
a peanut with a sprout.
George was puzzled.

Su amigo le mostró un cacahuate
con un retoño.
Jorge se sorprendió.

"This peanut grew into a plant,"
the man said. "Seeds and nuts
grow out of the ground, if they
are not eaten first."

—Este cacahuate se convirtió en una planta
—dijo el hombre—. Las semillas y nueces
crecen en la tierra, si alguien no se las come antes.

George thought he understood.
If a little peanut could become a big plant,
what would a rubber band become?

Jorge creyó que había entendido.
Si un pequeño cacahuate podía convertirse
en una planta, ¿en qué se convertiría una
liga de goma?

What would a feather become?

¿En qué se convertiría una pluma?

George dug lots of holes.
He buried lots of things.

**Jorge cavó muchos hoyos.**
**Y sembró muchísimas cosas.**

Soon the house was empty.
The man with the yellow hat
was surprised!

**Pronto la casa quedó vacía.
El hombre del sombrero amarillo
se llevó tremenda sorpresa.**

"George, umbrellas and chairs are not for burying," the man with the yellow hat explained.

—¡Pero Jorge!, las sombrillas y las sillas no se siembran —le explicó el hombre del sombrero amarillo—.

"They are made by people.
They are not going to grow.
Seeds and nuts will grow."

**Están fabricadas por las personas. No crecen.
Las semillas y nueces son las que crecen.**

A few days later George saw
something new in the yard.
It was a sprout!
"Look, George," said his friend.
"A seed you buried is growing!
I wonder what it will be."

**Pocos días después, Jorge vio
algo nuevo en el patio.
¡Era un retoño!
—Mira, Jorge —dijo su amigo—.
¡La semilla que sembraste está creciendo!
Me pregunto en qué se convertirá.**

Soon there was a beautiful
sunflower in the yard.
George had a green
thumb after all!

Pronto hubo un hermoso
girasol en el patio.
Después de todo, ¡Jorge era
un gran jardinero!

# YOU CAN DO IT

GEORGE DISCOVERS THAT NOT EVERYTHING GROWS . . .
BUT SOME THINGS CERTAINLY DO!

If you'd like to grow something, try planting beans. In a few days, you'll have bean sprouts! You may need to ask a grownup for help with this exercise.

1. Fill a jar or plastic cup with half a cup of dried beans (a grownup can find these at the grocery store).

2. Cover them halfway with cool water.

3. Place a piece of nylon or cheesecloth on top of the cup and secure it with a rubber band.

4. Put it in a shady place for eight hours.

5. Gently drain the water through the cloth covering. Then add more water and immediately drain again.

6. Return the jar to the shady spot you found, but this time rest it on its side to give the beans more room to grow.

7. Rinse the beans twice a day for the next three days (as in step 5). After that, the sprouts will be ready to eat in a sandwich or salad! AND YOU GREW THEM YOURSELF!

# WATER TRAIL

If you'd like to know how water helps a plant grow strong, find a piece of celery and some food coloring — then you can see for yourself!

1. Ask a grownup to cut a single stalk of celery for you that still has the leaves attached to the top.

2. Pick a food coloring (red or blue works best) and add some drops of it to a full glass of water.

3. Put the celery, leaves at the top, in the glass of water and leave it in a sunny place.

4. In a few hours, you might notice something different about the celery. Wait overnight.

5. The next day, check out your celery. It will be colorful! Ask a grownup to cut the celery in half for you. You'll see colored dots inside the celery. This is how you know water travels from the bottom of the stalk up to the leaf — the same way it travels up the stem of a flower—to help the celery grow strong!

Show what color your celery stalk became.